Andy Griffiths is one of Australia's funniest and most successful writers. His books have sold over 3 million copies worldwide, have been featured on the *New York Times* bestseller lists, and have won over 30 Australian Children's Choice awards.

Terry Denton is a Melbourne writer and illustrator of children's books who has collaborated with Andy Griffiths on 10 books. He loves the challenge of playing with Andy and finding new and exciting ways of entertaining their readers.

the BiG FAT COW that goes KA POW

BY
ANDY GRIFFITHS

ILLUSTRATED BY TERRY DENTON

SCHOLASTIC INC.
New York Toronto London Auckland
Sydney Mexico City New Delhi Hong Kong

ISBN 978-0-545-29666-3

Text copyright © 2008 by Backyard Stories Pty Ltd.
Illustrations copyright © 2008 by Terry Denton.
All rights reserved. Published by Scholastic Inc., 557 Broadway, New York, NY 10012, by arrangement with Feiwel and Friends, an imprint of Macmillan.
SCHOLASTIC and associated logos are trademarks and/or registered trademarks of Scholastic Inc.

12 11 10 9 8 7 6 5 4 3 2 1   10 11 12 13 14 15/0

Printed in the U.S.A.   23

This edition first printing, September 2010

Originally published in hardcover by Pan Macmillan Australia Pty Limited

Book design by Liz Seymour and Terry Denton

CONTENTS

BIG FAT COWS

It's raining
big fat cows
today.

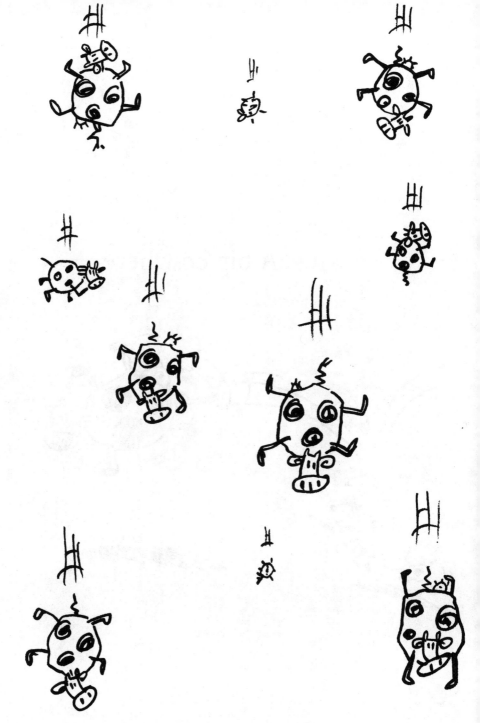

How many cows?
It's hard to say.

A big cow here.

A fat cow there.

Big fat cows are

EVERY

WHERE!

Cows underwater.

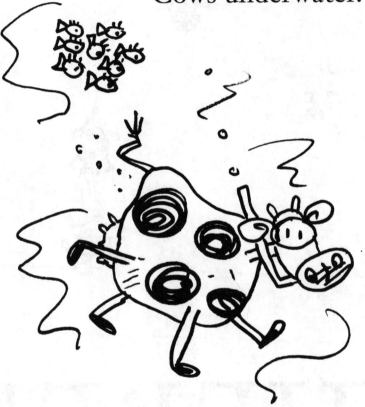

Cows in space.

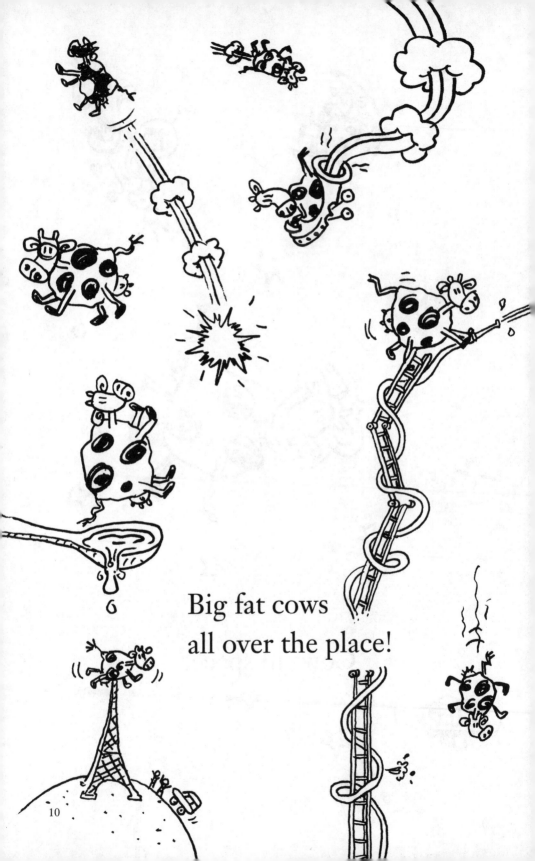

Big fat cows
all over the place!

6

10

Cows in boats.

Cows in suits.

Big fat cows
in cowboy boots!

This one is a
mixed-up cow.
It flaps its wings
and says meow!

Oh, no—watch out!

Don't look now!

This one is an

EXPLODING cow. . . .

NOEL THE MOLE

Here is a hole.

A deep,
dark
hole.

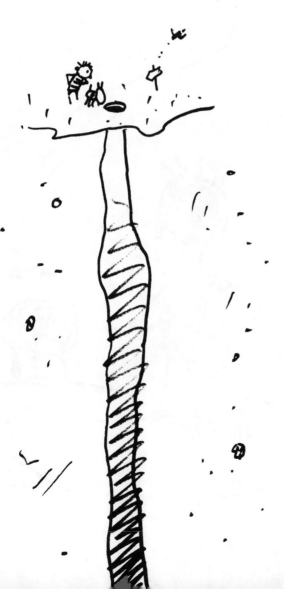

In this hole
lives a mole
called Noel.

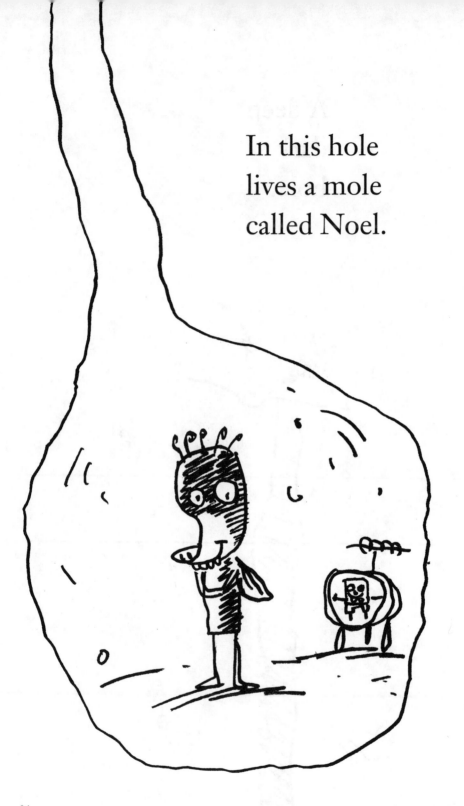

He eats
black coal.

He plays
rock and roll.

And
that's
the
whole
story
of
the
mole
called
Noel—
he's a
hole-dwelling,
coal-eating,
rock-and-roll
mole!

KLAUS THE MOUSE

This
is
Klaus.

Klaus
is a
mouse.

Klaus
the
mouse
has
a
very
small
house.

A
very,
very,
very,
very,
very

small
house.

But Klaus
the mouse
hates his
small house . . .

because
Klaus
is
a

VERY,

VERY,

VERY

BI

mouse!

WILLY THE WORM

This is Willy.
Willy the worm.

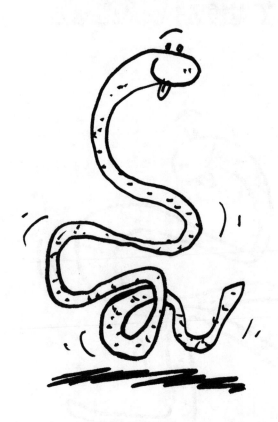

He goes to
squirm school
to learn how
to squirm.

But Willy the worm
is a very bad learner.

He's wiggly
on the
straight,

and a
terrible
turner!

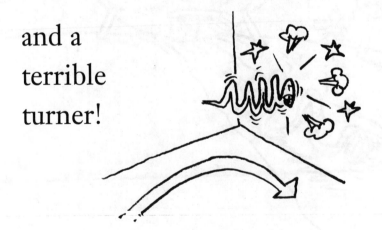

Willy never pays attention,
and he fools around a lot.

He always ends up
in a great, big knot!

KEITH, ED, AND DAISY

Here is a man
called Three-coat Keith.
He wears one coat on top
and two underneath.

Keith has a brother
called Five-hat Ed.

He wears five hats
on top of his head.

And this
is their sister,
One-dress Daisy.

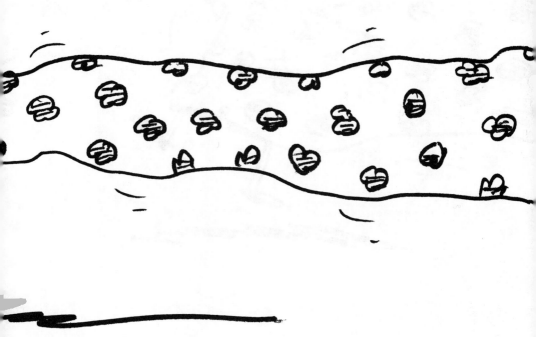

She shares her dress
with her best friend, Maisie.

LUMPY-HEAD
FRED

Have you heard
about the boy called
Lumpy-head Fred?

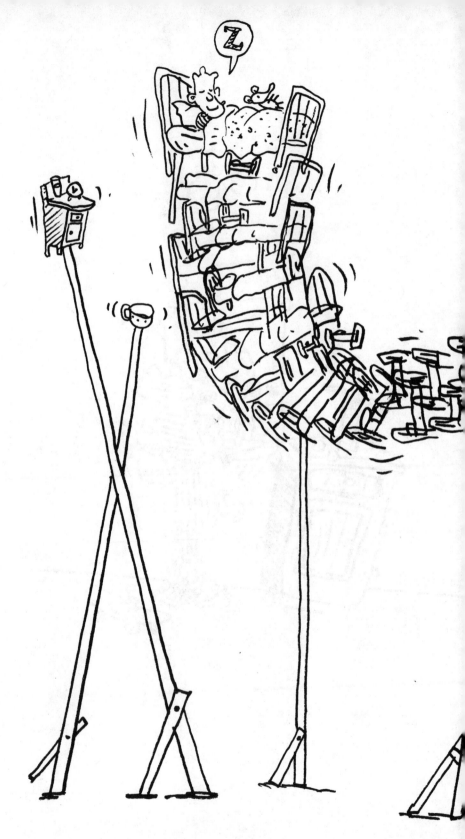

He sleeps
at the top
of a
100-decker
bed!

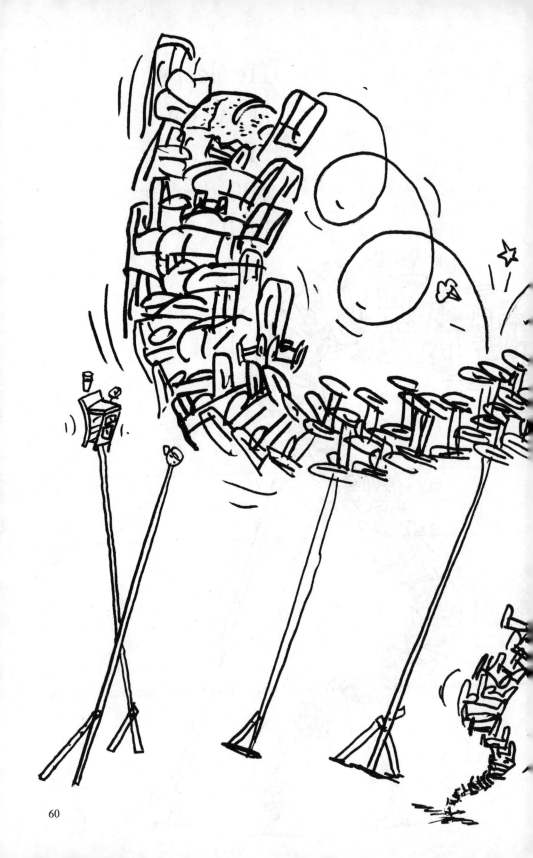

But
poor,
old
Fred
always
falls
out of
bed.

Which
is why
he has
such a
lumpy,
bumpy
head.

BRAVE DAVE

This is Dave
who, during the day,
is
REALLY,

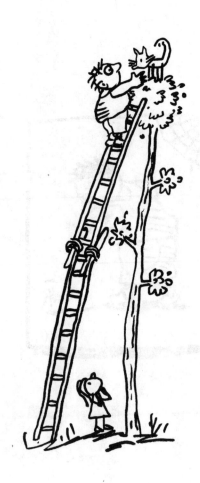

REALLY,

REALLY

BRAVE!

But during the night,
when there's no light,
Dave is NOT brave.
He takes fright.

Each noise
he hears
increases
his fears.

Every
BUMP,

every
THUMP

makes his
poor heart
JUMP!

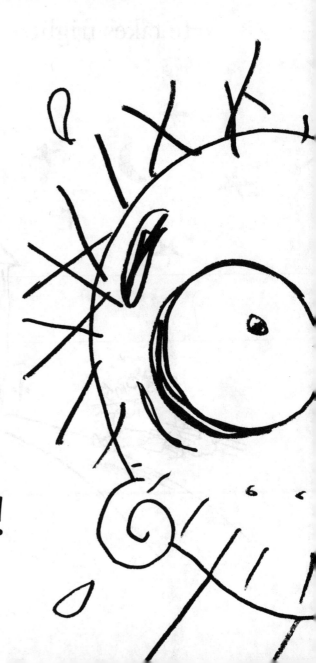

He sucks
his thumb.

He
calls
for
his
mum.

He can't wait
for the
morning
to come.

So, if you need
a brave job done,
call Dave in the day . . .

but at night,
call his mum.

RUTH'S SUPER SCOOTER

Here comes Ruth.
Ruth rides a scooter.
Ruth rides a scooter
with a super-loud hooter.

With a super-hoot here . . .

and a super-hoot there.

Here a hoot.

There a hoot.

Everywhere
a super-hoot!

We think Ruth
would be a LOT cuter
if she'd only stop blowing
her super-loud hooter.

MIKE'S BIKE

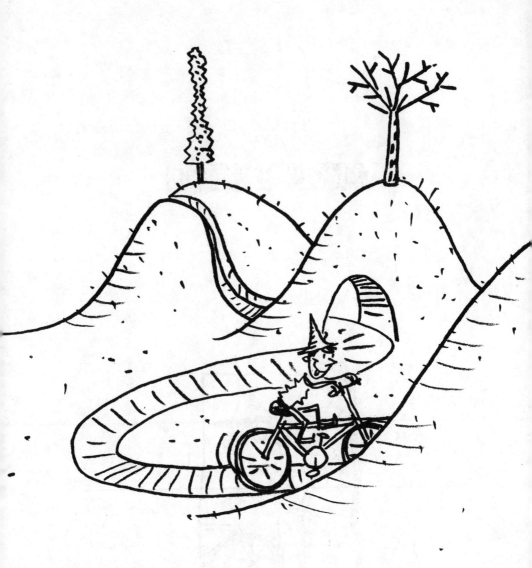

Here comes Mike.
Mike rides a bike.

Mike rides a bike
with a . . .

ve

ry

big

spike!

We don't like Mike
or his big, spiky bike.

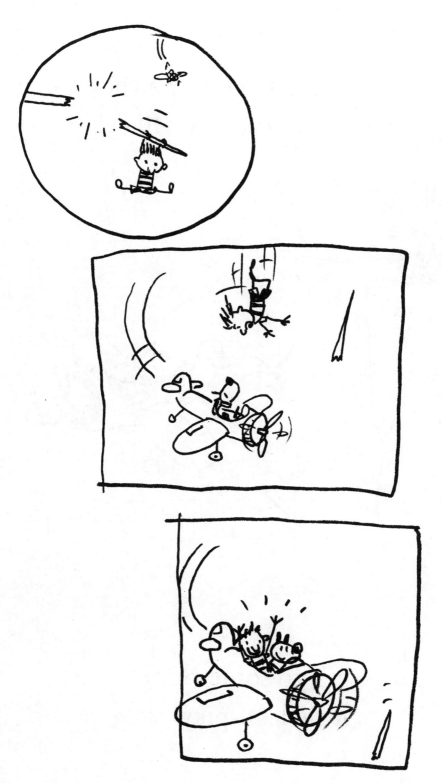

Let's go somewhere
a little less Mikey!

Let's go somewhere
a little less spiky!

SOMEWHERE LESS SPIKY

Here is a town
that is really incredible.
You can eat what you like
because
everything is edible.

Here is a sea
where you
can breathe
underwater.

You can stay
underwater
for an hour
AND a quarter.

Here is
a planet
where people
can fly.

And the clouds
are like
trampolines
up in the sky.

And here is a land
with big fat
rain.

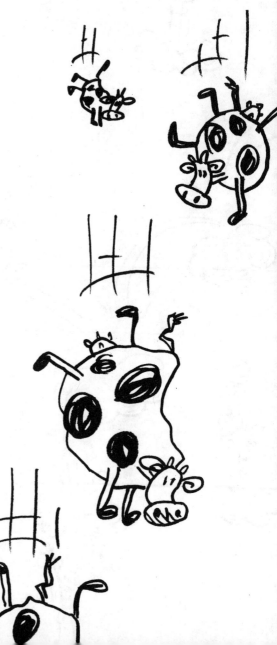

It's raining
big fat cows
again!

A big cow here.

A fat cow there.

Big fat cows are

EVERY

WHERE!

Oh, no—watch out!
Don't look now!
Here comes that
EXPLODING cow. . . .

The Friends who made
The Big Fat Cow that Goes Kapow
possible are:

Jean Feiwel, publisher
Liz Szabla, editor-in-chief
Rich Deas, creative director
Elizabeth Fithian, marketing director
Holly West, assistant to the publisher
Dave Barrett, managing editor
Nicole Liebowitz Moulaison, production manager
Jessica Tedder, associate editor
Caroline Sun, publicist
Allison Remcheck, editorial assistant
Ksenia Winnicki, marketing assistant